BOOKS MAKE GOOD PETS

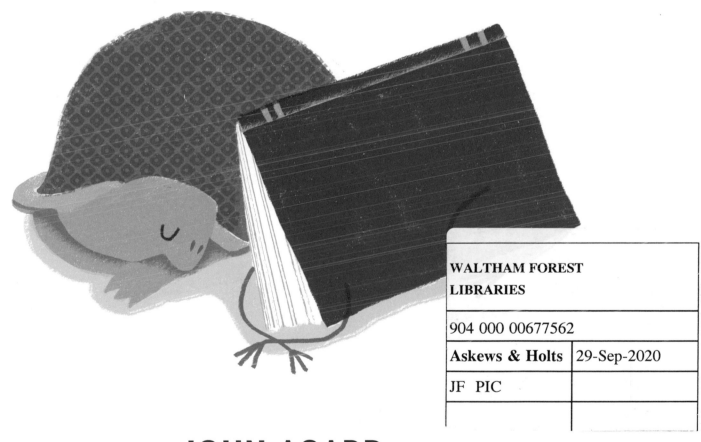

JOHN AGARD

illustrated by MOMOKO ABE

D1325509

WALTHAM FOREST LIBRARIES	
904 000 00677562	
Askews & Holts	29-Sep-2020
JF PIC	

WALTHAM FOREST LIBRARIES

904 000 00677562

Books make good pets
and don't need
going to the vet.

You don't have to keep

them on a lead

or throw them a stick.

They'll wag their words

whenever you flick

their dog-eared pages.

Even howl an ancient tale
for the
inward-listening ear.

Books make good pets
and don't need
going to the vet.

One curious look sets

their sentences purring

on the cushion of your eyes,
as if to say, dear browser,
you can pick me up

and throw me aside.
But one day you'll discover

I have more than nine lives.

Books make good pets
and don't need
going to the vet.

They'll burrow their way
through the dusty
reaches of your mind
to nibble at old ideas
and let in the new.
And you won't have to empty
any droppings on a tray.
No thank you.

Books make good pets
and don't need
going to the vet.

They'll hibernate
in the shell of their covers
and patiently wait
to be rediscovered
in their own good time
when some reader
rolls them over
on their cracked spine.

Books make good pets
and don't need
going to the vet.

They're easier to care for
than tropical parakeets.
They sometimes come in pairs
but prefer to breed in piles.
You don't have to feed
them sunflower seed
and just about anywhere
will serve as a nesting site.

From the perch of a shelf
they'll help you take flight
among the branches of yourself.

Books make good pets
and don't need
going to the vet.

They're as colourful as goldfish
in all their stillness. This is no whim.
Books can glow and swim . . .

in the bowl of
your imagination.

For my agent,
Caroline Sheldon
J.A.

For my 'Mama'.
Miss you for ever
M.A.

ORCHARD BOOKS

First published in Great Britain in 2020 by The Watts Publishing Group
First published in paperback in 2021

1 3 5 7 9 10 8 6 4 2

Text © John Agard 2020. Illustrations © Momoko Abe 2020

The moral rights of the author and illustrator have been asserted.

All rights reserved.

A CIP catalogue record for this book is available from the British Library.

HB ISBN 978 1 40835 987 7
PB ISBN 978 1 40835 988 4

Printed and bound in China

MIX
Paper from
responsible sources
FSC
www.fsc.org
FSC® C104740

Orchard Books
An imprint of Hachette Children's Group
Part of The Watts Publishing Group Limited
Carmelite House, 50 Victoria Embankment, London EC4Y 0DZ

An Hachette UK Company
www.hachette.co.uk
www.hachettechildrens.co.uk